For David, without whose words . .

Copyright © 1989 by Jan Ormerod
First published in Great Britain by Walker Books Ltd.
All rights reserved. No part of this book may be
reproduced or utilized in any form or by any means,
electronic or mechanical, including photocopying,
recording or by any information storage and
retrieval system, without permission in writing
from the Publisher. Inquiries should be addressed
to Lothrop, Lee & Shepard Books, a division of
William Morrow & Company, Inc., 105 Madison Avenue,
New York, New York 10016.

First U.S. Edition   2 3 4 5 6 7 8 9 10

Library of Congress Cataloging in Publication Data
Ormerod, Jan. The saucepan game / by Jan Ormerod.
    p.   cm. Summary: Baby and cat have a lot of fun
playing with a saucepan.
ISBN 0-688-08518-0. ISBN 0-688-08519-9 (lib. bdg.)
[1. Babies—Fiction. 2. Cats—Fiction. 3. Play—Fiction.]
I. Title. PZ7.0634Sau 1989 [E]—dc19
88-12893 CIP AC

The Saucepan Game

Jan Ormerod

Lothrop, Lee & Shepard Books
New York

Look at the saucepan.

Is there anything in it?

Lift the lid

and feel inside.

It's empty.

It has a handle . . .

and a lid.

What can you do
with a saucepan?

You can sit on it

like this.

Or you can hide in it

like this.

There's really nothing inside,

nothing at all.

Except a cat.

That's all.